Firespell
LOUISE COOPER

The Lost Brides
THERESA RADCLIFFE

DARK
ENCHANTMENT

The Hounds
of Winter
LOUISE COOPER

DARK
ENCHANTMENT

Kiss of the
Vampire
J. B. CALCHMAN

DARK
ENCHANTMENT

Valley of
Wolves
THERESA RADCLIFFE

DARK
ENCHANTMENT

Blood
Dance
LOUISE COOPER

In the DARK ENCHANTMENT series

Dance with the
Vampire

J. B. CALCHMAN

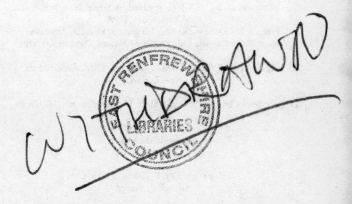

PUFFIN BOOKS

For My Parents

PUFFIN BOOKS

Published by the Penguin Group
Penguin Books Ltd, 27 Wrights Lane, London w8 5TZ, England
Penguin Books USA Inc., 375 Hudson Street, New York,
New York 10014, USA
Penguin Books Australia Ltd, Ringwood, Victoria, Australia
Penguin Books Canada Ltd, 10 Alcorn Avenue, Toronto, Ontario,
Canada M4V 3B2
Penguin Books (NZ) Ltd, 182–190 Wairau Road, Auckland 10,
New Zealand

Penguin Books Ltd, Registered Offices: Harmondsworth, Middlesex,
England

First published 1996
1 3 5 7 9 10 8 6 4 2

Set in 12/14 pt Sabon
Typeset by RefineCatch Limited, Bungay, Suffolk
Printed in England by Clays Ltd, St Ives plc

CHAPTER I

MASSACHUSSETS, USA
1995

'STOP! ALEX, STOP!'

He was deaf to her words. There was nothing else for it. Ella darted forward and tugged him away. Alex resisted but finally released his grip. The boy fell back on to the grass, out of the pool of moonlight.

'You took too much! I've told you before. Only take as much as you need.'

'Yes. You told me!' He turned away, cloaking himself in darkness. When he faced her again, he looked ashamed.

Ella took his face in her hands. 'The change isn't easy. I know that. But you must remember that you're not a killer.'

'I never realized vampires were so full of scruples,' he said.

'Not all of us are.' She shivered. 'There are others who leave a trail of death and destruction behind them. But there's no need.'

Letting her hands fall from his face, she knelt down to examine the boy. He looked as though he was sleeping. The incision had been precise and he would certainly recover.

'It's time we were going,' Ella said.

They made their way, hand in hand, back through the woods to the road.

'Do you ever regret being this way?' she asked as they climbed inside the silver Thunderbird.

He shook his head. 'What about you? Are you sorry you made me a vampire, after all the trouble I've been to you?'

'You're no trouble.' She smiled at him, running her fingers through his hair. 'It takes time to learn these ways.' She hesitated before continuing. 'I was so lonely before you came into my life. All that matters to me now is that we're together.'

He leaned towards her and kissed her. 'Thank you,' he said, 'I needed to hear that.'

He started the engine and pushed his foot down hard on the throttle. The car revved into life and they were propelled along the highway, hurtling through the dark night.

Ella was in the shower when she heard the door open. She shut off the water and reached for a bathrobe. 'Alex, is that you?'

As she came out of the bathroom, she gasped.

'What do you think?' he asked, removing his sunglasses. She looked up from his eyes to the top of his head. His hair had been cut to within a centimetre of his scalp.

'You look so different! Why?'

He shrugged. 'I needed a change. I thought you'd like it.' He set a paper bag down on the table. 'I bought coffee and doughnuts. Here, have one.'

She took the doughnut and removed the lid from the cup of coffee, watching the steam spiral to the ceiling.

It was a routine start to the day – waking in another motel someplace new, finding breakfast. Ella had lost count of the towns they had passed through. They had probably driven more miles in the Thunderbird in the past month than its previous owner had in years.

She glanced down at her bag. Souvenirs of their times in the States poured out on to the floor – postcards, coasters and snapshots. These flimsy bits of paper filled her with happiness, reminding her of conversations they'd had, places they'd been, things they had seen for the first time together.

'Ella, can we talk?'

She glanced up, snapping out of her daydream. Alex looked serious, tense. She had not seen that expression for a while. 'What's wrong?'

'It's time I went back,' he said. 'Charlie needs me. I have to go back to Oakport.'

'OK. Of course, I understand.' She was ashamed of the feelings of disappointment and jealousy. It wasn't right to feel jealous of Alex's family or to wish that, like her, he was all alone in the world. As they had travelled around during the past month, he had acted as if he had no cares and she had let herself believe it was true. Now, she had to accept that he had hidden his true feelings. Alex still had a brother and it was inevitable that he would want to return to him.

'Do you feel ready?'

'I'm as ready now as I'll ever be. Besides, the longer I leave it, the worse it'll be . . . for Charlie.'

'Have you thought about what you'll tell your aunt and uncle?'

He shook his head. 'Not really. I mean . . . obviously, I can't tell them the truth . . . the *whole* truth. Maybe you can help me come up with a convincing story.'

'Are you saying I'm a good liar?' She smiled at him playfully. But he wasn't in the mood for jokes. She adopted a more serious tone. 'Are you sure this really is the best thing . . . for Charlie and for you?'

'I can't leave him there.' Alex's voice was raw emotion. 'He's nine years old. He's my brother. I can't leave him with that man . . . the man who murdered our parents. Charlie can't protect himself. He needs me.'

What more could she ask? How else could she try to dissuade him? Now it was up to her. Should she go with him or end it here and now? For how could she tell Alex that, concerned as she was for him, an entirely different fear possessed her. A voice in her head – a voice long dormant – was warning her not to go to Oakport.

PRAGUE, 1782

PRINCESS ELISABETH TOOK a deep breath as she entered the ballroom. Her father – the emperor – had forbidden her presence at the ball. He thought her too young at fourteen to attend such an occasion. But there was no way she could stay away. It was her last chance to declare her love for Count Eduard de Savigny, before he left the court.

Thankfully, her older sister Anna had come up with a plan.

'Don't despair, Lissie – you shall borrow one of my dresses! And we'll all be wearing masks. You'll go in first – they'll all think it's me. I'll come along later once everyone's too involved in the party to notice.'

And so, here she was, entering the ballroom. She could hardly contain her delight as the waves of party-goers stepped back to bow and curtsy to her. She heard someone remark how graceful the Princess Anna seemed tonight. Little did they know it was really little Lissie in disguise!

The ballroom looked enchanting with flickering candles at every turn – some real, others reflections in the mirrors that lined the walls. Elisabeth glanced up above to the painted clouds that seemed to float across the ceiling. The cherubs sitting upon them looked as if they might shoot real arrows down into the crowd.

Elisabeth smiled to herself. The arrow of love had already pierced her heart. Since his arrival at court a month before, Count Eduard de Savigny had dominated her waking thoughts and, later, her dreams. But it was an impossible love. Tomorrow he would leave for Vienna to continue his experiments in alchemy. He would take with him both the gold and good wishes of the emperor himself. And, with them, the heart of a princess.

How many times had she watched him from afar at the dinner table? He was the most handsome man she had ever seen – his hair like long strands of gold, his eyes greener than the emeralds she wore around her neck. He was quite perfect.

And now she longed to find him in the crowd. But just as a mask hid her identity, so the masks around her made it impossible to tell who was who.

She was led on to the dance floor by a man who revealed himself to be a baron. He seemed keener to tell her about his livestock than to know anything about her. She could not have been more delighted when the music ended and she was released into the crowd. She wandered around, continuing to speculate which mask covered the face of her beloved.

'Have you found him?'

'Anna, is that you?'

'Of course!'

She hugged her sister but shook her head. 'No, I haven't found him yet. I've been too busy trying to solve Baron Kempinski's farming difficulties!'

Princess Anna laughed. 'He's such a bore. I believe he thinks the mere mention of his estate will melt a lady's heart. But now, let us see. Where can your count be?'

'May I have this dance?' The stranger's voice caught both sisters by surprise. Elisabeth waited for Anna to disappear with her suitor to the dance floor, but then she realized that the man was reaching out for her own hand.

Surprised, she returned to the dance floor. The man spoke little as they danced – a relief after the talkative baron. Elisabeth lost herself in the waltz music. As the music ended, she curtsied and began to walk away.

'Wait! Please . . . dance with me once again.' Flattered, she turned around. This time, as they performed the intricate steps, she noticed that he was watching her closely. She flushed with unexpected pleasure. They danced again and again. He was a fine dancer.

'Look, it's snowing!'

There was much excitement as the doors were opened and several couples ran out through them into the night air.

'Let's go outside.'

He took her hand and led her out through the door. They walked in silence towards the castle ramparts and gazed down over the city while eddies of snowflakes showered them from above.

'Take off your mask.'

His words filled her with fear.

'Please, I want to see your face. To see if you are as beautiful as I imagine.'

No man had ever spoken to her that way before. In spite of the cold night air, she felt her heart melting inside her. Suddenly, she wanted nothing more than to see the face of her mysterious suitor.

'I shall indeed remove my mask, but you must take off yours too. Yes? And I have one further condition – our identities must only be known to one another.'

'If that is your desire.'

He reached behind his head to unfasten his mask. She did the same. Her mask fell away.

'Princess Elisabeth!'

'You must not tell my father!'

But as his mask fell, all her fears receded. She found herself looking into the face of Count Eduard de Savigny. He smiled and lowered his head to kiss her. Could this really be happening? Maybe her love had finally led her into madness.

But no, he spoke. He asked her to walk with him. And so they left the castle and the music behind them, walking on towards the bridge. Towards the white, deserted city.

As they reached the bridge, he stopped and drew her towards him. He planted the sweetest of kisses on her lips and cheeks, beneath her ears and down the curve of her neck.

Elisabeth stroked his golden hair, looking up to the eddies of snowflakes. Suddenly, she felt a searing pain as if twin blades had punctured the base of her neck. And yet, as the pain gave way to numbness, she was powerless to do anything but watch the falling snow.

'What have you done? What have you done to me?'

He did not answer, but merely raised his bloodstained mouth in a strange smile.

CHAPTER II

OAKPORT, MAINE

THEY ARRIVED IN Oakport just after nightfall. The town was quiet. As they drove along the edge of the ocean, Ella could make out the dark surface of the churning water. Suddenly a beam from the lighthouse swept over the waves. Then the light was gone and the dark returned.

'Is it far to Shadow Street?' Ella asked.

'Let's not go there tonight,' Alex said. Ella was surprised but relieved. 'We're both tired,' Alex continued. 'Let's get some sleep and head over there tomorrow.'

'Where are we going to sleep?' Ella asked.

'The boathouse,' Alex said. 'We'll sleep at the boathouse.'

He turned the Thunderbird away from the main road on to a narrower track. There were fewer and fewer houses along this way. Pretty soon there was scarcely any sign of habitation at all and they were driving through a corridor of thick black spruces.

Ella felt a sudden chill. She was tired and

hungry. And she somehow still feared what awaited them here in Oakport.

At last, the forest thinned out and they were heading towards water again. This time it wasn't the ocean but a lake. The placid waters contrasted strongly with the churning surf she had glimpsed before.

Alex brought the car to a standstill besides a wooden boathouse nestling at the edge of the lake. He switched off the ignition. Ella wished they could have continued driving. As long as they were moving, they were free.

There was a padlock on the door. Alex crouched down on the ground, searching among the stones. He pulled out a key and opened the door.

He took a book of matches from his pocket and struck a match. The tiny light sparked and died all too quickly. He struck another match, shielding it from the draught. This led him to the hurricane lamp. A third match lit the lamp. There was still oil inside it and the lamp filled with light, illuminating the room. 'I'll get our bags,' he said.

Ella was left alone in the room. There were dust sheets on the chairs. She lifted one. It floated away like a ghost. She removed the other sheets and piled them in a corner.

Alex had told her all about his family and the happy weekends they had spent here. The evidence of those times was everywhere. On the shelves, scores of old paperbacks nestled by battered boxes of Monopoly and Twister. There were maps and other guides to the woods, and framed family photographs. As she took in all the Culler family's possessions, she heard Alex's voice retelling his story.

We were a close family. Before Ethan Sawyer came into our lives. Before even Aunt Sarah moved back from the West Coast. It was just Mom and Dad and Charlie and me, then. Just a regular family doing all the regular things. Most weekends, we'd go trekking in the woods. We often stayed at the boathouse. It was my grandfather's. It was like a second home to me.

We didn't have the boat then – not a proper one. It was Ethan who got us into all that. Before him, we just had a small rowing boat. Sometimes I'd take Charlie out in it and we'd fool around on the lake. Mom was always worried about him.

When Sarah came back East, everything changed. She came along with us on a camping trip. After that, she was with us every weekend. And then she met Ethan and he came along too. I guess we enjoyed having them around. Mom certainly liked Sarah's company.

It all happened so fast. One minute, we were getting to know Sarah all over again. The next, Ethan Sawyer rolled right into our lives. And just as we were starting to make sense of it all, they

13

went missing for a weekend. Turned out they'd flown to Vegas and got married.

It was the same when Ethan bought the boat. He just drove us out to the harbour and it was waiting for us. After that, we spent our weekends on the ocean. Dad had always been interested in sailing and Ethan said that he should treat the boat as his own – that we all should. He said it was his gift to us for letting him into our family . . .

She could see them now – like a snapshot come to life: Charlie sitting on the rug, playing cards with Alex; their dad and Ethan poring over a chart, plotting out the sailing trip, and their mother and Sarah sorting out food supplies in the kitchen.

The picture faded as Alex brought their bags into the room and closed the door behind him. 'We'll stay here tonight. I'll see if there's any food left in the kitchen.' Ella was unnerved by Alex's composure. It was as if nothing terrible had happened – as if his mother and father had never died – and his only worry was what to cook for supper.

She followed him into the kitchen to find him already pulling cans of food from the larder. 'It's not gourmet but we'll make do,' he said. 'I'm starving. Are you ready to eat now?' She nodded, although she had no appetite, and he began opening up the cans.

She left him in the kitchen and returned to the living room. Again, she imagined the Cullers as they had once been and how they might have welcomed her among them, excited to meet Alex's new girlfriend.

'Why don't you go out on to the deck?' Alex called from the kitchen. 'There's a fantastic view of the lake.'

On one side of the room, there were double doors leading out on to the deck. Ella opened them and stepped out into the cool evening air. The lake was a dark indigo now. A small rowing boat was moored to the deck. Ella watched it bob on the inky water. Alex's words flooded back to her.

We should never have gone out that day. The coastguard forecast a storm late in the afternoon. Ethan said we'd have plenty of time to go out and return by then – we'd been planning the trip for weeks, we couldn't waste the chance now. And so, we set off. Mom and Dad and Charlie and Ethan and me. Sarah stayed at home – she was helping out with some bake sale or something . . .

At first it seemed like great sailing weather. There was just enough of a breeze and the sun was strong. As soon as we left the harbour it began to get rougher. Out past the headland, Mom wanted to turn back – she was worried that Charlie would get sea-sick. Ethan said that we could ride it out – that Charlie was a natural sailor. Of course, Charlie agreed. Dad told Mom not to worry – that Ethan knew what he was doing.

The storm hit suddenly – earlier than forecast. Ethan tried to turn the boat around, but the gale was too strong for him. Dad and I tried to help but we were thrown back and forth across the boat. I remember Mom trying to keep hold of Charlie. The boat was bouncing on the water and we were all clinging on for our lives.

The next thing I knew, I was in the water and the boat was on top of me. Everything seemed to happen in slow motion then. I could see our stuff sinking down to the ocean floor. Somehow, my life jacket had come loose and I realized I'd have to swim my way back up. When I surfaced, the boat was a wreck. I couldn't see any of the others.

Then Ethan and Charlie went past in the dinghy that we kept at the back of the boat. Charlie looked unconscious. Ethan was rowing him ashore. I thought he was going to come back for me. I swam around, trying to keep calm, searching for my mom and dad. I called out to them but they didn't answer. I guess I lost track of time.

It was like a dream – a nightmare. The sea water was icy cold and I was getting more and more confused. I wasn't sure I could keep treading water much longer.

Then, something snapped inside me. I knew that if I didn't start swimming, I would never make it ashore. In spite of my numbness, my arms and legs took over, propelling me towards the land. And I left my parents to die . . .

'Supper's ready.' Ella shuddered as his voice, his hand on her shoulder, brought her back from her imaginings.

'Are you all right?' he asked. 'You look very pale.'

She found it difficult to understand how he could be so calm. 'Doesn't it disturb you being back here?'

He shook his head. 'Not really. We had so many great times here. I feel I'm close to my family again. I know it's weird but I feel like they're here with us.'

Later, after they had washed up the dinner things and closed up the house for the night, Alex took the hurricane lamp and led the way upstairs.

'Wait!' Ella said, her eyes settling on one of the photographs. It was half-hidden behind several others and veiled in dust. As Alex brought the light back towards her, Ella brushed the surface of the glass clean. She looked down at the picture. 'That's him, isn't it?'

Alex nodded. 'That's him – the man who murdered my parents.'

In the picture, Ethan Sawyer was sitting in a

dinghy, between Alex and Charlie. One of Ethan's hands was resting on Charlie's shoulder, the other waving at the photographer. All three of them were smiling.

He had thick, pale blond hair and deep blue eyes and looked younger than his thirty-five years. He was strikingly handsome – not at all what she'd expected from the picture Alex had painted.

She found herself drawn back to his eyes, which seemed to come right out of the photograph, as if he was talking to her. She rested the picture back down on the shelf beside the others.

But later, out of the depths of sleep, Ethan Sawyer's face returned to her. She found herself transfixed by his gaze. This time, he was holding out his hand to her.

She sat bolt upright with the shock, as if she had dived into freezing water. Now she realized how right she had been to fear their arrival in Oakport.

PRAGUE, 1782

'COME HERE,' he said. With one hand, he held back the branches and with the other reached out to help steady her balance on the rough ground.

She took his hand gratefully and he drew her close beside him.

'Now look.'

She stared through the gap he had made through the branches, into the glade. A boy was standing there. She turned to Eduard, confused.

'What's he doing here in the forest?'

'Not so loud!' he whispered in reply. 'He might hear us.'

It was then that she noticed a peculiar light emanating from Eduard's eyes. Simultaneously, her own heart began to thud. She looked back at the boy. Her initial feelings had been concern for his safety. But now her anxiety about him wore off, replaced by an altogether different sensation.

'Don't fight it,' Eduard whispered in her ear, as if he had read her mind. 'Let the hunger flow through you.'

His words had the power of command over her. She felt her body give itself over to this feeling – shockingly alien but at the same time perfectly natural.

The rest happened in a blur of speed. Before she knew it, she was inside the glade itself. Eduard had the boy in his arms and had punctured his frail neck. She watched, fascinated.

Her body was on fire. Eduard looked up at her, his eyes brimming with light. She could not wait any longer.

She crouched down beside him. She saw the puncture marks already beginning to close. No. That mustn't happen. Not before she too had her fill. Without further delay, she dug her teeth down into his neck and waited.

Nothing happened. She felt a burning sense of dissatisfaction – a fear that her hunger would be unfulfilled. And then it came. The rich blood seemed to explode like fireworks on her tongue. It raced into her mouth and down . . .

She could not stop, would not stop. Only by taking more could she sate her needs. And yet, as she drank, the need seemed only to grow stronger, deeper. She feasted until at last she was overcome by exhaustion and fell back on to the ground.

When she came to, she did not recognize her surroundings. She was still in the forest but not in the glade. She looked around curiously, noticing the reflection of the moon on the water. She was at the side of a small lake.

'I brought you here to clean yourself,' Eduard said.

To clean herself. What did he mean? She pulled herself to her knees and looked down into the water. She drew back, terrified. She had seen a devil lurking beneath the water's surface.

Then her heart began to pound. Slowly, she looked down again and saw her own face. It was dirty with blood.

Her thoughts turned to the boy. Now the hunger was gone and her thoughts were once again for his safety. She gazed up at Eduard. 'Where is he? We have to get back to him . . . to help him.'

Eduard shook his head. 'It's too late.'

'No!' She opened her mouth to scream but the word emerged as a hoarse whisper. She looked down once again at her own reflection. 'What have I done? What kind of monster am I?'

CHAPTER III

A S SHE DRESSED the following morning, Ella found herself shaking. The voice deep within her was telling her to turn and run but she couldn't leave Alex to face this alone – especially if what she feared was true. Whatever the danger to herself, she had to stay with him.

Alex was tense. He didn't speak during breakfast, except to check this or that detail of his story. Finally, he glanced at his watch. 'Shall we go?'

By daylight the lake looked quite different, thought Ella, glancing behind to the water as they drove back into the forest. For the first time, she was able to see across to the other side of the lake. Alex's voice returned to her.

I came to late in the night. At first, I couldn't remember what had happened. Then it hit me – the churning waves, all the pain, all the loss. In the darkness, I couldn't tell where I was. Then I must have lost consciousness again. When I next woke, it was morning. I was tired and hungry.

When I finally found the nearest town, I realized I was way up the coast. We'd driven through

*the place once or twice. There was a gas station.
I went into the washrooms. I could see in the
mirror that I was a mess. There was a deep
wound just below my neck. I cleaned myself up
as best I could and hitched a ride back towards
Oakport.*

*When I got back to town, I saw the newspaper.
The lead story was about the accident. It
reported that three bodies had been found.
My dad's, my mom's and a third. It was more
beaten up than the others but presumed to be
mine. As far as they were concerned, I was
dead.*

*Ethan was quoted saying all kinds of things.
That he'd taken the dinghy around and around
trying to find us and only then gone back to
shore. That he'd broken down when he recognized my sweater on the body. He was lying. And
that made me think. What if this wasn't an accident after all? What if he wanted us to die? All of
us, except Charlie?*

As they neared the peak of the cliff, the church
came into view, swimming in a sea of graves.
'This is the place, isn't it?' Ella asked. Alex
nodded, bringing the car to a standstill.

They walked through the gateway and round
past the church. Ella felt she had been here
before. She seemed even to know where the
graves were. She crouched down to read the
inscriptions.

Adam Culler, 1952–1995. Beloved husband of Charlotte and father of Alexander and Charles . . .

Charlotte Baines Culler, 1954–1995 . . .

She turned to the last grave, knowing what to expect. Still the words chilled her.

Alexander Culler, 1978–1995. Son of Adam and Charlotte. 'In their death they were not divided' . . .

'Look! Someone brought me flowers,' said Alex, leaning across her to pick up a bunch of tattered roses. The petals fell from the stems and were carried away on the breeze. Ella watched them until the specks of colour disappeared from view, swallowed by the blackness of the spruces at the cliff-edge.

I watched the funeral from the edge of the churchyard. I was cold and tired and my wound throbbed. I wanted to run to Charlie – to show him I was still alive. But I knew I couldn't trust Ethan Sawyer.

Neither Ella nor Alex heard the car door close. The sound was drowned out by the noise of the wind in the trees. The voices too were muffled by the breeze. It was only as Ella turned that she saw the couple closing the gate and walking out towards the graves. Alex had seen them too. He looked suddenly panic-stricken.

'What is it? What's wrong?' Ella asked.

'Quick! Get down!' Alex pulled Ella back to the ground. He looked frantically from left to right.

'Over here!' He began crawling towards a pair of large headstones, a few rows back. Ella followed, her hands and knees scraping the wet grass. As she started to understand what was happening, her heart began to pound. They reached the cover of the stones just as the couple came to a stop a few rows away.

'It's a good thing I brought fresh roses.' The woman's voice was close now, clear. Ella thought she could hear the flowers being removed from their wrapping.

'I'll take that, shall I?' This time it was the man. Ella could tell from the sounds that followed that they were arranging the flowers on the graves.

'They won't last long in this wind,' said the man.

'That doesn't matter. I just want them to know we're thinking about them. That we still . . .' She broke off, overcome by tears.

The man spoke softly. 'Not an hour goes by when I don't think about that day. If only I had been quicker, had done more. If only I had saved them . . .'

Ella glanced at Alex. His dark expression confirmed her suspicions. The man and woman were Ethan and Sarah Sawyer – Alex's uncle and aunt.

'You couldn't have done anything more,' Sarah said – the words pushing through the tears. 'At least you saved Charlie. And I'm sure they're all grateful for that.'

'I just wish . . . I just wish I could have saved . . . if not Adam and Charlotte then at least Alex. He was only seventeen. That's no age . . .'

Ella turned to Alex again. He was frowning. Perhaps he too was confused. It certainly didn't sound like Ethan had wanted him to die.

'I'd give anything to have him back,' Ethan said.

Ella saw the effect of the words on Alex. It was as if he had been put into a trance. He stood up slowly, deliberately, until he reached his full height, and stared, unblinking, at Ethan.

Ella heard Sarah let out a wail. Ella raised her eyes above the gravestone and saw Ethan Sawyer in the flesh for the first time.

His long, golden hair was like a flame in the dark churchyard. His eyes were fixed on Alex. 'It's a miracle!' Ethan said, approaching Alex and hugging him. Tears streamed from his eyes. Alex remained inanimate.

Sarah too moved towards Alex. Ethan stepped back, making room for her, smiling through his tears.

'Is it really you?' Sarah's voice was weak. She held out her hand, the tips of her fingers making contact with Alex's face. Hesitantly, she traced the outline of his jaw. 'Welcome back,' she said, hugging him. 'Welcome back.'

For the first time, Alex's face gave way to emotion. Ella saw him hug Sarah back. They remained in each other's arms as the wind swept around them. Ella watched them, sensing that Ethan's eyes were fixed on her. She willed herself not to look at him. She was not yet ready for this. Would she ever be?

At last, Ethan rested his hand on Sarah's shoulder. 'Let's take Alex home.' Sarah reluctantly drew back but one hand still clutched Alex tightly.

'Come on,' she said. 'I'll take you to the car.'

Ella felt suddenly exposed and abandoned. She knew that Ethan Sawyer was watching her but she still jumped when he spoke.

'I'm not accustomed to meeting people in churchyards.'

It was him. Of course it was him. He looked a little different in this incarnation but there was not a trace of doubt in her mind.

'I'm Ethan Sawyer,' he said, offering his hand. Why was he pretending? They both knew who he was.

She did not take his hand. She looked away. Alex and Sarah had almost reached the church gate. She began to run after them but her movements were sluggish. In a moment, he was at her side. He looked at her, sadly.

'Why do you always run from me, Elisabeth?' he asked.

She stared up into his eyes. At once, she felt the familiar dizziness. She lost all sense of where she was, feeling herself pulled backwards into a tunnel through time. All around her, old scenes replayed from their times together. Now she was walking across the African plains. Now, wandering through the gardens of an Italian villa. Now, ordering drinks in a French café. And always with him. Over two hundred years and still it seemed she could never leave him. Further and further back through the centuries she journeyed, until once again she heard the waltz music and looked down to find herself in the green ball gown.

CHAPTER IV

'**C**OME ON INSIDE,' Sarah said, unlocking the door. 'I'll make us some coffee.'

While Sarah busied herself in the kitchen, the others waited in the living room. It was spacious and simply furnished. On the walls were stunning black and white photographs. They were all nature studies – grasses wet with dew, moss-covered bark and driftwood in the surf. Ella read the signature in the corner of each frame – *Ethan Sawyer*.

'They're wonderful, aren't they?' Sarah said, bringing out a tray of mugs. 'You should see Ethan's new exhibition. It's spectacular.'

'Where's Charlie?' Alex asked abruptly. Sarah immediately fell silent.

'He's at school, Alex,' Ethan said calmly. 'Where else?' He poured a mug of coffee and handed it to Ella.

She took the mug, turning away from his eyes. 'Don't fight it.'

He hadn't spoken but the words were clear inside her head. Ella began to shake. She couldn't control it. The hot coffee began to seep over the sides of the mug, spattering over Ella's jeans and down on to the floor. Finally, the mug itself slipped from her grasp and dropped on to the rug.

'I'm so sorry.' Ella rushed towards the kitchen, but Sarah had already grabbed a damp cloth.

'It's nothing,' Sarah said, mopping up the liquid. 'We're all shaken up. After everything that's happened today, how could we not be? Here, give me the mug. I'll fill it up for you.'

Sarah handed a fresh mug to Ella and went to sit beside Alex on the sofa. Ella's hand was steadier now. She had to pull herself together – for Alex's sake.

'So, Alex,' Ethan said, 'where do we begin?'

Alex took a deep breath as he began the story he'd so carefully rehearsed. 'I was found up the coast by fishermen, near Archangel Point. They took me to the hospital. It was three days before I regained consciousness. By then, my wounds were starting to heal. I stayed at the hospital a full month . . .'

'Which hospital?' Sarah asked.

'The one up near Archangel Point . . .' Ella saw that Alex was looking nervous.

'I don't remember there being a hospital up there.' Sarah looked to Ethan, but he did not respond.

'It's only a small hospital,' Alex said.

'Why didn't they contact us?' Sarah said.

Alex looked down at the palms of his hands. 'I told them not to.'

'You did?' Sarah looked hurt.

'I wanted to make sure I was fully recovered before I came back for . . . to Charlie.'

Ethan nodded.

'I don't understand.' Sarah seemed torn between tears of anger and rage. 'It's as if you *wanted* us to think you were dead.'

Ella studied Sarah's face. It was a strange face for a woman in her mid-thirties, at once innocent as a child's yet etched with worry-lines. Alex had told Ella that Sarah had gone through a bad time before she met Ethan. Ella wondered what Sarah's life was like now. How much did she know about Ethan? And how did Ethan treat her?

'Where are you staying now?' Ethan asked.

'Out at the boathouse.'

'How did you two meet?' Sarah turned suddenly to Ella.

'At the hospital.' Ella shifted in her chair as she relayed her part of their elaborate lie. 'I was visiting my cousin. She was in a road accident. She was in the next bed to Alex. We got talking and soon became . . . friends.'

'But you're not from here.' Sarah took a sip of coffee. 'Your accent . . .'

'I'm English, but I have an aunt and uncle out here. I've been staying with them for the summer.'

'Do they live around here? Maybe we know them?'

Ethan laughed. 'We don't know absolutely

everyone in Maine, hon. I think that's enough questions for now, don't you?'

'Of course.' Sarah nodded, hugging Alex.

'When will Charlie be home?' Alex asked.

'Oh, not for another few hours,' Ethan said, looking at his watch. 'He has a violin lesson after school. You remember, Alex, how important his music is to him.'

'I can't wait to meet him,' Ella told Sarah. 'Alex has told me so much about him.'

Ethan looked from Ella to Sarah to Alex. 'I think it's best if we talk to Charlie first; prepare him. I'm still reeling from seeing you again. Imagine what it will be like for him.'

Alex frowned. 'I want to see him . . . as soon as possible.'

'Of course,' Ethan nodded. 'We'll talk to him when he gets home.'

'I want to see him,' Alex repeated, standing up. 'I want him to know that I'm . . .' He caught Ella's eye. 'That I'm . . . back.'

Ethan also turned to Ella. 'I'm sure *you* agree, Ella. It's better not to rush things.'

Unnerved, she walked over to Alex and took his hand.

'Go back to the boathouse,' Ethan said. 'We'll speak to Charlie and tell him you'll come over tomorrow.'

'Maybe they'd be more comfortable at a motel?' Sarah said. 'If it's a question of money . . .'

'No,' Alex interrupted. 'We'll be fine.'

They walked out into the hallway. Alex turned to leave but Sarah wouldn't let him go before she had hugged him again.

Ethan held out his hand to Ella. She took it, nervous of making physical contact with him.

'It was good to meet you,' he said, 'And I want to thank you.'

'What for?' Ella asked, surprised.

'For bringing Alex back,' Ethan said.

Although his tone remained even, his grip tightened around her hand, not letting her move until he released her, silently reminding her how powerful he was. She trembled. If there was one thing she had learned over the years, it was not to cross this man. Yet that was what she had done by bringing Alex back. And he was only too aware of it.

PRAGUE, 1782

PRINCESS ELISABETH OFTEN dreamed of her family and of the life she had left behind. More than anything, she wanted to go back. But with the passing of each day, the possibility of escape seemed ever more remote.

Living in the forest, she felt no different to the wild beasts who roamed its pathways. By day, she wandered around – trying to come to terms with her own savagery. But by night she stalked her prey with an eager anticipation and, increasingly, deadly precision.

Eduard seemed pleased with her company. Thinking of the dashing figure he had cut at court, she was constantly amazed to see him live this way – stalking this wilderness like a jungle cat. Yet in spite of the strangeness of this world and the transformation they had both undergone, she was still drawn to him – in many ways, more strongly now than ever.

But he told her that they would soon leave the forest. He was making plans to return to his castle in a neighbouring province. Elisabeth felt a flush of excitement at the idea of once again living within walls and sleeping on a plump mattress rather than the rough forest floor. But leaving the forest meant leaving Prague far behind and closing for ever the door to her past life. Eduard had told her before that she could never go back.

'Absolutely not. I forbid it.'

'But I only want to say goodbye.'

He laughed coldly. 'They won't even let you through the castle gates looking the way you do now.'

It was true, she supposed.

'At least let me see the castle one last time.'

He shook his head. 'It's for your own good. We'll talk no more of this. I have to make plans . . .'

His arrogance was beyond all bounds. If he did not want something to be, he simply shut all possibility of it out of his mind. But in her own head, the thought of returning home did not fade so easily. As Eduard busied himself with 'plans', she roamed through the lonely forest, picturing herself back within the labyrinthian castle chambers.

She reached out for the trunk of a tree, imagining it to be one of the columns in the castle ballroom. She made believe that the bird song was orchestra music and that, once again, she was on her way to the dance. She was still wearing her ball dress, she reminded herself, even if it was in tatters now and blackened by spatters of mud and blood.

The daydream would not go away. She knew

that, whatever Eduard said, she had to go back. She was sure she would be all right if only she could make it as far as the gates. She knew the guards by name. They had always had a soft spot for the emperor's daughters. One of them would be sure to recognize her and let her back inside.

And so, she too began to make plans – noting, by the shifting patterns of light, the times when Eduard left her alone. Exploring the furthest reaches of the forest, she determined the quickest route out. And one morning as Eduard left her, casually remarking that he would be gone a matter of hours, she set off.

She had found that, among the changes in her physical being, she could move much faster than before. She felt exhilarated by her speed and this new mastery over her body, convinced that she was heading towards her salvation.

As she hurried through the rain-slick streets, she became increasingly aware of her ragged appearance. Dusk was falling and she was glad that the deepening shadows hid her shame.

At last, she crossed the bridge just beneath the castle. Her heart beat faster and faster as she began the climb to the castle gates.

The guard ignored her at first, thinking that she had only come to beg. When she called him by his name, he stopped dead in his tracks and a strange look passed over his face.

'I can't explain now, Lajos,' she gasped, 'but

just let me inside so I can see my father. I'll see you're rewarded.'

'Princess Elisabeth!' he rasped, a rebel tear sliding over his rough skin. 'Just knowing you're safe is all the reward I need.'

He opened the gate and she stumbled inside, tears of relief flooding down her dirty cheeks. As the gate closed behind her, she glanced back, and her heart suddenly lurched within her. Eduard was there on the other side of the gate, fixing her with furious eyes.

She froze, terrified. His mouth was closed and yet she heard his voice clear and loud inside her head. 'You can never escape from me. You can never run away from what you've become.'

'You're shivering.' The old guard turned her back towards the castle. 'We must get you inside into the warmth.'

CHAPTER V

'HE'S TRYING TO stop me seeing Charlie.'

Ella watched Alex pace the length of the living room once again. He'd been this way all afternoon – ever since they'd arrived back at the boathouse.

'No,' she said calmly, 'he just wasn't there.'

'Maybe we should have waited.'

Ella touched him gently on the arm, stopping him in his tracks. 'You can't keep torturing yourself like this. You'll see him tomorrow.'

'I know.' Alex shrugged as she slipped her arms around his waist. 'It's just I've come so far . . . waited so long for this. I just wish I knew everything was going to be OK.'

'Everything's going to be fine.' She kissed him. 'Why don't we go for a drive?'

'Where to?'

'Since when did we need anywhere special to go? Let's just get in the car.'

They drove along the cliff road, watching the sun sink down into the dark ocean. Alex seemed to lose himself in the action of driving, his hands and mind fixed on the wheel. Ella felt the cool breeze running through her hair. She shivered. She could not get Ethan Sawyer out of her mind.

After a while, the cliff road turned inland and they found themselves driving through a more built-up area. Ella watched Alex as he manoeuvred the Thunderbird through the streets. His face was marked with grim determination. She wondered if he was lost but something stopped her from asking.

She turned to look at the houses to one side of the street. The street lamps illuminated broad gardens sweeping down to the road. Alex slowed the car and Ella caught a good look at a house where a party was going on. One of her favourite songs was playing and inside the building people were dancing.

At first she did not realize that the car had stopped. She was transfixed by the view into the house. A tall, blonde-haired girl was dancing in the centre of the room. She was a great dancer, pretty too. A couple of guys tried to get her attention. She danced with one for a moment or two, but soon turned away. When the other approached her, she smiled and did just the same. Ella liked her style.

As the song ended and the girl moved out of view, Ella glanced at Alex. His eyes were still fixed on the lighted window. Ella realized in a moment that it was no fluke that they had ended up in this street, outside this very house.

She hesitated before speaking. 'Do you want to go inside?'

Alex smiled softly. 'Are you suggesting we crash the party?'

'I get the impression you know the people inside.'

Her heart beat fast as he turned towards her and met her eyes. He seemed surprised but relieved. 'Yes,' he said, 'I know her . . . at least I did.'

A car roared up beside them. They both turned as the driver manoeuvred it wildly into a space on the other side of the street. A young couple got out from the car. They were obviously on their way to the party. The girl began walking towards the front door, but the guy caught her, drawing her into a kiss. As she pulled away, she looked straight at Alex and Ella. Her face paled and her eyes narrowed in on Alex.

Alex too seemed shaken. But in a moment he managed to collect his senses and switch the engine on again. He steered the Thunderbird back into the centre of the street. As they drove away, Ella glanced back at the girl. She was waving her hand towards the car and crying out words Ella could not hear. Her boyfriend held her back. Then, Ella lost sight of them as Alex turned the car out of the street.

They raced back towards the lake. Before the road broke off towards the boathouse, Ella nudged Alex.

'Stop the car.'

'What?'

'You heard me. Pull over. Just here . . . by the lake.'

He followed her instructions, bringing the car to a standstill at the water's edge.

'Now, get out of the car . . . No! Don't turn off the ignition, just get out.'

He was confused but did as she said. She leaned over and flicked on the radio, twisting the dial until she found a rock and roll station. She turned the volume up.

'Let's dance,' she said, walking towards him and reaching for his hand.

His movements were awkward at first. Perhaps he felt self-conscious too. But he soon started to loosen up.

After a couple of up-tempo songs, the DJ slowed it down. Ella and Alex danced close together, their movements becoming ever slower and more slight. Then, he pulled her closer still and their mouths met.

Afterwards, she took his hand and they sat down on the bonnet of the car.

'Do you want to talk about it?' she asked.

'I don't know what to say,' he said.

'I've been there,' she said. 'I know what it's like. On the outside, looking in.'

He nodded.

'You feel like the world you used to be part of is out of your reach. Like the people you once knew are trapped on one side of the window and you're on the other – all alone.'

'Yes. But I'm not alone.' He lifted her mouth towards his and kissed her again.

As he drew away again, she asked the question that would not go away. 'The girl – the blonde that was dancing – she was more than just a friend, wasn't she?'

'Her name is Carrie . . . Carrie Jordan. We went out for a while.' He looked sad. Ella felt that, in spite of all he had said, he would do anything to have his old life back again.

'Did you love her?' Why was she doing this to herself – asking the very questions that threatened to hurt her most?

'I guess I did . . . in a way.'

He saw that she was upset. He reached for her hands and looked deep into her eyes. 'It was all very innocent. We went to the movies and parties and . . . we had fun together. But it was kids' stuff compared to the way I feel about you. I want to be with you always. Whatever happens now, it's you and me.'

She slipped her hands free and reached up to his shoulders. They kissed with more intensity than ever before.

'How about you?' he asked her as they parted. 'Have you been in love before?'

His question took her by surprise. 'Come on,' he persisted, 'tell me or I'll tickle you!'

She was not in the mood for jokes. She

shrugged off his hands and turned away, looking down into the deep, inky waters of the lake.

'I'm sorry, Ella. I was only fooling around. You don't have to tell me . . . if you don't want to.'

'No.' She turned back towards him. 'No. I do want to.'

'Then what's wrong?'

'It's a long story. I first met him a long time ago.'

'How long?'

'Two hundred years ago.'

'What was his name?'

'He called himself Eduard de Savigny *then* . . .'

'Very grand!' She was aware that it must all seem like a fairy tale to him.

'He was a count,' Ella continued. 'But then I was a princess.'

Alex was clearly intrigued. 'What do you mean that he called himself de Savigny *then*?'

She paused before continuing. 'He was a vampire, Alex. He was the one who made *me* a vampire. He was called de Savigny then, but he has had many other names since . . . as have I.'

'I don't understand.'

'It's called "blood possession". I only became Ella Ryder a couple of years ago. I drained Ella of her blood and my . . . "spirit" – I guess that's what you'd call it – transferred into her body.'

'So what would happen if you were to drain someone else's blood?'

'Then, providing I got it right, my spirit would enter that person's body.'

'And what would happen to the original Ella?'

'It depends,' she said, carefully. 'Things can go wrong. It's not something we do for fun. But every now and then, there is a reason to assume a new identity.'

'So this de Savigny, he's still out there . . . in a different body?'

She nodded.

'Imagine.' Alex's mind was working overtime. 'Imagine if you were to meet him . . . oh, no, of course, if he was in a different body, you wouldn't recognize him.'

She was about to correct him, to tell him that it didn't matter what you looked like on the surface – you could still recognize one another. But she couldn't go on.

'I wonder where he is now,' Alex said, unable to let it go. 'I wonder who he is.'

CHAPTER VI

ETHAN OPENED THE door to them with a smile. He took their coats and beckoned them through into the living room.

'I hope you were OK at the boathouse,' Ethan said pleasantly. Ella nodded, without looking him in the eye. 'Can I get you a drink?' he asked, heading towards the kitchen. 'Coffee or a coke or something?'

'Where's Charlie?' Alex asked.

'Sorry,' Ethan called from the other room, 'did you say you *would* like a drink?'

'I said, where's Charlie?' Alex said.

'He'll be down in a minute. He's just finishing his scales.' Ethan turned to Ella to explain. 'He's a very dedicated violinist. He's come on leaps and bounds in the past few months.'

Alex opened his mouth to say something but Ethan disappeared into the kitchen. Alex and Ella's eyes met. She could tell what he was thinking. And she agreed. This was pretty weird.

'Hello,' Sarah arrived in from the garden, holding a bunch of flowers in her hand. 'What a beautiful morning!' she said, kissing first Alex then Ella.

Again, Alex and Ella's eyes met. She knew that

his patience was running out. He strode out of the room and headed for the staircase. She decided to follow.

As they climbed the stairs, they heard the music. It was hard to believe it was a boy of nine playing it. The sound was very smooth and melodious but there was an extra quality – a depth of feeling.

Charlie was standing in the centre of the room, his back to the doorway. He carried on playing, apparently unaware of their presence. Ella watched the emotion flood into Alex's face.

The music ended. Charlie stood in position for a moment. It was as if the music had not quite left him. Alex and Ella waited. Finally, Charlie turned towards them.

'Alex. They said you were coming by.' Charlie's voice had almost no expression.

'Charlie . . .' Alex seemed struck dumb. As Charlie began packing away his things, Ella pushed Alex into the room. He walked up to Charlie and took his hands away from the violin case, catching them in his own and kneeling in front of him.

'I came back for you, Charlie,' Alex said, hugging his brother. 'I've missed you so much.'

Charlie looked up, over Alex's shoulder, at Ella. He seemed embarrassed. 'Did you like the music?' he asked.

'You're a very talented violinist,' Ella said.

'That's not what I asked,' he said. 'I asked about the music.'

She was taken aback. He had piercing eyes and did not speak like a nine-year-old.

'It was very haunting,' she said.

'Haunting.' He weighed the word. 'Yes, I like that. I made it up myself, you see. I'm Charlie, by the way,' he said, approaching her with his hand outstretched.

'Ella,' she said. 'I'm Alex's friend.'

'I like you,' he said, as if he had given the matter great thought. 'I like you heaps better than Carrie.'

He brushed past her and headed for the stairs. Ella watched Alex pull himself up and walk towards her. His face showed the confusion he was experiencing. What was happening?

They walked down the stairs to find Charlie had joined Ethan and Sarah in the living room. Charlie was sitting beside Ethan on the sofa and telling him about his new composition. 'I'm going to dedicate it to you,' he said decisively.

'Well now, since we're all together,' Ethan said, 'I think it's time we told Alex and Ella our news.'

'Yes!' Charlie grinned, wrapping his arm around Ethan's waist. Even Sarah seemed to be brimming with excitement.

Ella took Alex's hand. His eyes looked empty now.

'It's quite simple, really,' Ethan said. 'We're going to adopt Charlie.'

'We've already started the procedures,' Sarah added. 'Isn't it wonderful?'

Ella felt Alex's shock. She looked from Sarah to Charlie and then to Ethan. They looked like the perfect, all-American family. It was as if they had managed to erase the horrific events that had brought them together and created themselves anew.

Alex clenched her hand tightly and began pulling her towards the door. She was only too willing to follow.

'Alex! Ella! Wait. Don't go.' Sarah chased after them. 'What's wrong? Let's talk about this.'

Ella glanced back. Alex did not turn. He got into the car and started the engine.

'There's nothing for me here,' Alex said bitterly. 'We're leaving Oakport.'

She leaned over and kissed him sadly. He would never know it but he had saved her. Just in the nick of time.

CHAPTER VII

'I CAN'T BELIEVE what's happened to Charlie,' Alex said, as they packed up their things. 'We were so close.'

Ella caught his hands. 'You have to face it, Alex, he does seem to be happy with Sarah and Ethan.'

Alex shrugged. She could see tears welling in his eyes. 'I guess you're right.'

She clasped his hands tightly. 'Maybe it's time for us to get on with our own lives, Alex. We're just beginning.' She looked into his eyes. 'We're going to have such a wonderful time together.'

'Yes.' He smiled, but could not hold back the tears any longer. She pulled him close and let him cry into her shoulder.

It was hard for her to maintain the pretence of feeling calm when really she was terrified that he would change his mind about leaving Oakport. She knew now that she could not remain in the same town as Ethan Sawyer. As long as he was around, she would never be free to start over. Every time he looked at her, she became that frightened young girl again, alone in the snow. She had to move on – to break free of the memories, both good and bad, that flooded back every time she saw him or heard him speak.

'Hello! Anybody home?'

They both recoiled at Ethan's voice. In a moment, he was standing just behind Alex, smiling at Ella. 'I'm sorry to crash in like this, but I think we need to talk.'

There was no way Alex could hide from Ethan the fact that he had been crying. Ethan raised his hand to squeeze Alex's shoulder but, at the last moment, thought better of it.

'Sarah insisted I come,' Ethan said, sitting down on the sofa. 'She was upset that you stormed out of the house like that. We all were. I wanted to explain –'

'You may as well know, we're leaving town tonight,' Ella said.

Alex glanced at her in surprise, but Ethan seemed to take this news in his stride. 'I hope I can dissuade you from making that journey.'

He stood up and walked over to the bookshelf, picking up the photograph of him in the boat with Alex and Charlie.

'That was a great trip, remember, Alex?' he said, smiling. 'I guess they all were. Look, I know this adoption stuff has taken you by surprise. It *is* very sudden, after everything that's happened but Sarah and I feel it's really important to get things back on track.'

He held the photograph out to Alex. 'Look at him. He's smiling. And I want him to smile again.'

'Oh, he seems perfectly happy,' Alex said, bitterly.

'Alex, we're adopting Charlie because he needs people to take care of him ... You're seventeen – old enough to look after yourself. But not old enough to easily look after him.'

He sat down again, this time on the arm of the sofa Alex was sitting in. 'Stop by the house again tomorrow. Say around noon. Spend some quality time with Charlie ... just the two of you. We want you to stay a part of this family ... your family.'

Ella's heart and head were pounding. She had to put a stop to this. But how could she, without revealing to them both the depth of her feelings for Ethan?

Ethan put his arm around Alex's shoulder and hugged him. 'You coming back is a miracle, Alex. And miracles don't happen too often in Oakport. Don't throw this wonderful chance away. What do you say?'

Alex seemed incapable of arguing. His body seemed suddenly drained of all strength. As Ethan drew back his arm, Alex slumped against the corner of the sofa. His eyes were closed.

Ella looked at Ethan with alarm. 'What have you done?'

'Nothing,' Ethan said. 'He's very tired. It's been quite a day for him. For us all.'

He stood up again. This time, he moved differently – prowling around the room as if he owned the space.

'I think you should go,' Ella said, not quite as fiercely as she intended.

Ethan considered for a moment. 'I'm sure you wouldn't mind me staying for just one drink.'

Ella stood up. 'You shouldn't drink and drive. We don't want another tragedy, do we?'

They were standing face to face now. Ethan stared into her eyes. 'What could possibly happen to me?' he laughed. 'All right, I can see you're not in the mood for talk tonight. Well, I'll look forward to seeing you tomorrow. And while Charlie and Alex are getting reacquainted, maybe we should spend some time together alone.'

He turned and swaggered out of the boathouse. Ella looked at Alex, sprawled over the sofa. Her anger bubbled. She ran out after Ethan. He was about to climb into the car but stopped when he saw her.

'You can't keep doing this,' she cried. 'Every time I get myself back together you come after me and turn everything upside down again.'

He looked at her with amusement. 'That's hardly fair. This time you came to me. And you know, you're more beautiful than ever.' He traced the curve of her cheek with his finger.

She was still shaking long after he had reversed the car out on to the street and driven off into the night.

PRAGUE, 1782

A S SHE AWAITED an audience with her
father – the emperor – Elisabeth's joy at
returning to the palace was tinged with
feelings of fear.

Her mother had prevented Elisabeth from seeing the emperor until she had cleaned herself up.
In the meantime, she was conducting her own
interrogation.

'It was Count de Savigny, yes? I saw you out on
the castle wall.' There was a coldness to her
mother's voice – a distance. Elisabeth knew what
her mother must be thinking had happened.
How her head would spin if she knew the truth.

A nervous, young maid hovered around them,
smoothing the creases from a stunning sapphire-
coloured dress. Elisabeth looked at herself in the
mirror. She thought she looked older even
though she had been absent only a matter of
weeks. And yet there was a new flush to her.
Although she had felt herself to be close to
death, she looked more alive, more vibrant than
she could remember.

'I'll wait for you in our chamber,' her mother
said, slipping out of the room.

Elisabeth dipped her arms into the blue satin

dress the serving girl held over her and scooped up two necklaces from the jewellery box before her. One of the necklaces was gold, the other a string of sapphires. She was uncertain which to wear. The serving girl stepped back, waiting for the princess to decide.

Watching the way the gold necklace caught the light, Elisabeth thought of what story to tell the emperor. Should she let him believe, as her mother clearly did, that Eduard had simply deflowered her? What would life have in store for her then? The gossip would penetrate through the thick castle walls and bring shame upon the emperor and his family.

And yet . . . and yet. She held the string of sapphires close to her neck. Perhaps she could tell him the truth. Her father was a man of experience. He had travelled far and wide and was benefactor – and friend – to all manner of alchemists and adventurers. Perhaps he would know about such things as this. Perhaps he even knew of a cure.

'I'll wear the sapphires,' she decided. The serving girl stepped forward to help her fasten the chain. Elisabeth couldn't help but notice the swan's arch of the girl's neck. She followed the arch down to where it met her narrow shoulders. The now familiar hunger surged inside her . . .

No! Not here! Not now. She tried to still the hunger but it was too powerful. Before she knew it, she had the girl's throat in her grip and was biting down into her neck . . .

Breathless, she let the girl's body fall to the carpet. Now what? She looked in the mirror once again and lifted a lace handkerchief to wipe away the blood around her lips. She caught herself in the process. There was no turning back. She realized then that she must leave the castle for ever.

She flung open the door of the chamber and ran out into the corridor. She heard her parents' voices but hurried past their room, hurtling down the great staircase and across the hall. The solid wood doors were impossibly heavy but her strength was gaining all the time. She tugged them open and charged out into the cool night.

As she neared the gates, she heard a familiar voice. 'It's all right. I have made plans.'

She looked up and saw a carriage and horses, waiting just beyond the gate. The guard looked sadly at her but opened the gate all the same. She clasped his hands for an instant but there was no more time to lose. The carriage door opened and another hand reached out to help her inside. As the door closed behind her, the horses tore off into the night.

She turned towards Eduard. He was clean and dressed in new clothes, looking more elegant and handsome than ever before. She scanned his face for signs of anger but found none.

*

She awoke from a deep sleep to find herself in his arms. The carriage had come to a halt and she looked out through the window to see a magnificent castle bathed in the soft moonlight.

'This will be your new home,' Eduard said, lifting her down from the carriage. 'Come inside.'

He took her hand and led her into the hallway. A few servants paused from their duties to smile and call out in welcome. They seemed pleased that their master had returned. There was an air of warmth and informality about the place.

'Come,' he said, leading her up the stairs and along a corridor. They came to a door, just slightly ajar. He urged her to push it fully open. She did so and found herself inside a ballroom. Around the edges of the dance floor were candles flickering atop all manner of candelabra.

'Now, dance with me,' he said.

'There's no music.'

But suddenly, she heard the first stirrings of her favourite waltz. She glanced around the room, seeking out the source of the music. She could see no one playing. Her eyes returned to Eduard and she thought she understood.

Gratefully, she fell into his arms and let him lead her to the centre of the floor. She lost herself in the music and the thrill of his touch, feeling her heart flood with joy. The light of the candles seemed to dance around her. She smiled.

'I love you.' Shocked, she looked back into his

deep, green eyes. This time, she really wasn't sure if he had spoken the words or if her mind was simply playing tricks upon her.

CHAPTER VIII

'I HOPE I got your size right,' Ethan said, smiling. 'Go on, Alex. Aren't you going to try yours on?'

Alex looked at Ethan as if he had asked him to walk on fire. He glared at the Rollerblades, sitting inside their box. But Charlie had already buckled his up and Ethan was helping him on with his pads.

'Now, Charlie,' he said, 'the guy at the store told me you have to promise not to do this without wearing pads, you understand?' Charlie nodded and raced off down the road.

Ethan watched him go. 'You'd better get a move on, Alex, or Charlie will be out of sight!' Ethan turned to Ella. 'I'll just grab my car keys and we can get going too.'

'Where are you going with him?' Alex asked, buckling his blades.

'To the gallery,' Ella said.

'The gallery? You're not seriously interested in his photographs, are you?'

'Don't worry about me, Alex. Just give it your best shot with Charlie, OK?'

He nodded and leaned forward to kiss her. As he did so, he lost his balance. They both laughed.

'I guess these blades are going to take some getting used to,' Alex said and skated off after Charlie.

Ethan reappeared with the keys. 'All set?' he asked Ella.

She nodded and walked over to Ethan's car.

As they drove away, Ethan slipped a CD into the car stereo. 'How long's it been?' he said. 'Thirty years? Forty?'

She shrugged.

He shot her a smile. 'Don't say you're not pleased to see me?'

She shrugged.

'You're looking very well,' he continued. 'This Ella suits you.'

He looked almost the same as he had the first time she had met him – a little older, rather more American than European. Blue eyes instead of green but equally intense. His hair was the same colour and was a similar length, falling down to the base of his neck.

He smiled at her. 'We've got a lot of catching up to do.'

She wanted to hate him – out of loyalty to Alex, and to make him pay for the past. It was easier said than done. There were good memories as well as bad. She felt her pulse quicken and her fear give way to a sense of anticipation.

Ethan turned off the road into a small parking

lot, beside the lake. He brought the car to a standstill.

'How far are we from the boathouse?' Ella asked.

'It's on the other side of the lake,' he said. 'This place was a boathouse too. But we've made some changes inside . . .'

'I thought you were just exhibiting here.'

'Sarah and I own it,' Ethan explained. 'Come on inside!' He opened the door for her.

Ella walked into the exhibition room. It was large, empty of furniture, and wood from floor to ceiling. It was as stark as it could be, perfectly setting off the photographs that hung on its walls. Like the boathouse, the building opened straight out on to the lake.

Ethan led her from one picture to the next, telling her about the locations and the way he'd achieved particular effects – the story behind the pictures.

'You've come a long way,' she said, adding with a smile, 'since Paris!'

He caught the joke and laughed with her. 'I think I was a little avant-garde even for the French.'

A few more people strolled into the gallery. When they realized Ethan was the photographer, they'd start up a conversation. But Ella could see that Ethan was not in the mood for this. It did not surprise her when he took her arm and led her to the door.

'Let's go and get some lunch,' he said. 'I want some time alone with you.'

'Something's bothering you,' Ethan said over lunch, 'tell me about it.'

'I want you to make peace with Alex,' she said.

'Talk to *him*,' Ethan said, reaching for the lobster tail. 'He's the one who insists on making me the enemy.'

'Does he have any reason to do that?' she asked. Their eyes met.

'What are you accusing me of?' Ethan asked.

'Alex says that you murdered his parents.'

Ethan closed his hand over Ella's. 'It was an accident,' he said. 'Oh, I was stupid, pig-headed – well, you know what I'm like! I should have paid more attention to the storm reports.'

Ella looked deep into his eyes, trying to decide if this was the truth. He returned her stare.

'Look, I saved Charlie, didn't I?' he said. 'And I looked for Alex for hours. I didn't know he'd swum to safety.'

She wanted to believe him so very much.

'Why would I jeopardize everything I have with Sarah by killing her brother and his wife? What could I possibly have to gain?'

'You really love her then?' Ella had forgotten all about Sarah. She felt a flash of guilt at hearing her name.

When she glanced up at him, he was smiling at her. It was not the smile he had offered to the people at the gallery. It was a genuine smile, full of warmth, full of love.

'I've missed you,' he said.

She turned and looked at him, filled with fear and sorrow and longing. And then his lips met hers and she forgot everything but the longing.

CHAPTER IX

S ARAH WAS STANDING in the doorway as Ethan's car pulled up at Shadow Street.

'You were gone such a long time,' she said as he kissed her hello.

'I took Ella to the gallery and then we got some lunch. We started talking and, well ... I guess we have a lot in common.'

Sarah smiled weakly at Ella. Ella felt uncomfortable. She was about to ask if Charlie and Alex were still out blading, when she heard a trail of violin notes from upstairs.

'Is Alex up with Charlie?' she asked.

'Oh no.' Sarah shook her head. 'They got back ages ago. Charlie went up to his room and Alex drove back out to the boathouse.'

Alex opened the door to her but said nothing.

'I'm sorry I'm so late,' she said.

'Gee, that's all right,' he came right back at her. 'I can quite understand why you'd want to spend the afternoon with my psychotic uncle.'

She hadn't expected him to be this angry. 'How was your day?'

'Great, thanks,' he said sarcastically. 'My little brother was on excellent form – just a joy to be with. He's so happy with his new life with Ethan and Sarah. What does it matter to him that his parents are six feet under or whether I'm alive or dead?'

Ella sat down at the other end of the sofa. He had every right to be upset.

'Nice Rollerblades, huh?' Alex lifted the blades and spun the wheels. 'Uncle Ethan's spoiling us, don't you think?'

Something snapped inside Ella. She felt guilty, angry and confused. 'Give him a break. You can't blame Ethan for everything that's happened. You have to face the fact that Charlie *is* happy with them. Maybe he should stay here while we get on with our own lives . . .'

'Only it isn't exactly a life, is it?' Alex said. 'Let's not forget that my name's on a gravestone out there in the churchyard. Oh and by now, I've probably been given another funeral in England. So when you come to think of it, I don't have too much of a life to be getting on with.'

He stormed out on to the deck. Ella followed. She tried to push down her anger. She had to keep calm.

'He told me about the accident, Alex,' she said, reaching for his shoulder. 'He admits he should have brought the boat back earlier. He feels really guilty. He did come back to save you but he couldn't find you. It was misty.'

Alex shook his head. He would not accept this

version of events. She looked into his eyes, hoping in vain.

'Have you finished?' he asked, coldly. 'Does the defence for Ethan Sawyer rest its case?'

She was incensed. 'I'm not defending him! I'm just . . .'

'You seem quite convinced by his side of the story,' he snapped, shrugging her hands from his shoulders.

It was growing dark, the lack of daylight intensified by gathering storm clouds. Ella glanced down into the dark waters of the lake.

She tried once more to change his mind. 'But when you think about it, Alex, what *he* is saying fits with your version of events. It isn't a question of sides . . .'

Alex would not give in. 'He identified my body for the police, remember? He told them that yes, it was me lying on that slab . . . when I was upstate, in a hospital bed being fed soup. He organized my funeral while I was buying a plane ticket to England. How does he explain that?'

She had no answer for him. She felt a chill come over her. It wasn't just the first icy droplets of rain. Ethan hadn't told her the truth . . . at least, not the whole truth. There was still more she needed to know.

'I . . . have . . . to go.' She darted inside. The keys to the Thunderbird were on the table. She scooped them up and raced out of the door, leaving her coat and bag on the sofa. Alex ran after her. It had started to rain.

'NO!' he called, racing to the car. But she was too quick for him. Before he reached her, she stamped down hard on the throttle and sped away along the road.

Sarah answered the door. She was clearly surprised to see Ella again. 'What do you want?'

'I have to see Ethan,' Ella said.

'He's rather busy just now,' Sarah began but in a moment Ethan himself came to the door.

'You look awful,' he said. 'Come in and get dry.'

She shook her head. 'No. You come with me.'

'Ethan,' she heard Sarah say, 'what exactly's going on?'

Ella turned and walked back towards the car. Ethan chased after her. He had scarcely fastened his safety belt as she drove away at high speed.

'Where are we going?' he asked.

'You're not the only one who can spring a surprise,' she said, enjoying the feeling of power.

He leaned back against the seat and looked out of the window. Ella grew tired of the game. She needed answers.

'Why did you say the body they found was Alex's?' she asked.

He took a moment. She turned, expecting him to be smiling, smugly. She was shocked to see the way he looked – scared and doubtful, vulnerable even. She was not accustomed to seeing him like this.

'I really thought it was Alex,' he said. 'The face . . . the face was too badly . . . damaged. You couldn't tell. But he was Alex's height and build. He had long, dark hair. Most of his clothes were torn up . . . except the scraps of his shirt. I thought I recognized the shirt . . .'

As he broke off, Ella stole another glance at him. Tears were streaming down his face.

'Ella, watch the road!' he cried.

As she turned, she saw that the car was veering perilously close to the cliff edge. She tried to bring it under control but they were travelling much too fast and the road was narrow and winding. They were heading towards a deep precipice.

Alarmed, she wrestled with the wheel, managing to pull the car away from the edge just in the nick of time. She slowed the Thunderbird and, as the road widened, brought the car to a standstill.

'Now what?' he asked.

'I want you to come back to the boathouse,' she told him. 'I want you to tell Alex what you've told me. I want an end to this feud tonight.'

The boathouse door was ajar and the floorboards nearby were wet with rain. The hurricane lamp was unlit and the clouds blocked out all light from the moon. As her eyes adjusted, Ella could see that the living room was empty.

She was about to call out to Alex when she noticed that the doors to the deck were open. The flimsy curtains flapped like streamers in the wind, spraying the room with droplets of rain.

She stepped out on to the deck. Her foot came up against something soft but firm. She glanced down and realized that there was a human body stretched out at her feet.

Just then, the moon broke free of the storm clouds and the boathouse was bathed in light. Ella recognized the body below her. It was the girl who had recognized Alex outside the party. She looked up, helplessly, at Ella. At the very least she was unconscious. Instinctively, Ella lifted the damp strands of hair and saw the puncture marks on the girl's neck.

There was a crash in the living room. Ella turned. The hurricane lamp had fallen to the floor. Alex stood above the mess of broken glass. He moved towards her, as if sleepwalking. His shirt was torn and spattered with blood.

'Why here?' Ella asked, numbly. 'Why did you bring her here?'

'I couldn't help it. She saw us out blading. She must have followed me.'

'You've taken too much blood, Alex. I warned you . . .'

'I was angry,' he said. He was shaking.

'I think you've killed her.' Ella stepped inside

out of the rain. As she did so, Ethan, who had been standing beside her on the deck, crouched down to inspect the body.

'What's he doing here?'

'It's OK,' Ella told Alex. 'He understands.'

She saw Alex make the connection. The pieces to the jigsaw came together in his head.

'She's going to be all right,' Ethan said. 'We just need to get her out of here.'

But Alex just stood there, staring at Ethan. 'You're one of us,' he said. 'You're a vampire.'

CHAPTER X

THEY LEFT THE still unconscious girl at the side of a road, leading out of the woods. In the morning, someone was sure to find her. There would be no way of tracing what had happened back to the boathouse.

'But what happens when she remembers that she followed me here?' Alex asked.

'She won't remember anything for a few days,' Ethan said. 'And when she does, it will all be confused. Besides, who would believe her? Everyone around here thinks you're dead.'

Listening to them, Ella felt a sudden sense of relief that the truth was out in the open. She wondered which of them was the more surprised – Alex at discovering that Ethan was a vampire, or Ethan at discovering that Alex was.

Back at the boathouse, Alex went to clean himself up, leaving Ella and Ethan alone in the living room. Alex was wide awake now and seemed ashamed of what he had done.

Ethan smiled. 'So, you have an apprentice of your own.'

'You should go,' Ella said, abruptly. She didn't want to talk to Ethan about Alex.

Ethan did not move.

'Sarah will be worried,' Ella said.

Ethan glanced at the clock. 'I suppose you're right.' He held out his hand. 'Walk with me to the car.'

She followed, anxious to see him go. But as soon as they were outside, he grabbed her by the shoulders, bringing her face to face with him.

'What are you doing with Alex?' he said harshly.

'I love him,' she cried, trying to wriggle out of his grip. She couldn't.

'No.' Ethan shook his head. 'It isn't love.'

Ella looked angrily into Ethan's eyes. How did he know how she felt about Alex? What right did he have to storm back into her life and tell her whom she loved and whom she did not love.

'Don't you see?' he continued. 'It isn't over between us.'

'It has to be. I'm with Alex now. And you're with Sarah.'

'I don't love *her*. How could I feel about her the way I do about you? Sarah and Alex are like children. You and I . . . we're different. We've seen so much, been through so much *together*.'

That was true. They had shared a lot of history. *You can never escape from me. You can never run away from what you've become.* He had spoken those words 200 years ago. Then, they had seemed only a threat. But now, she knew it was true.

She had spent 200 years running from him and from the way he lived – taking whatever, whoever he wanted and never mind the cost. Leaving a trail of death and destruction behind him. She had been sure that there was another way, had taught herself moderation. But now everything was uncertain again.

She thought she had found a new beginning in Alex. So much so, that she had brought him back from the realms of the dead. But even by bringing him back – making him a vampire – she had only succeeded in creating another monster. She had tried to teach him to control his hunger, just as she had taught herself. But it was no good. Alex's bloodlust showed every sign of being as insatiable as Eduard's. Maybe that was just the way it had to be. Maybe it was time for her to accept that there was no escape from blood. Death and destruction were just a part of the deal.

She looked up into Ethan's eyes. As she did so, their blueness seemed to fade, replaced by the emerald-green of Eduard de Savigny.

'We'll talk again soon,' he said. 'You'll see I'm right.' He started up the car and disappeared into the night.

Ella found Alex out on the deck, sitting as still as a statue. The rain had died away to no more than a drizzle but there was still a cold wind. He did not seem to feel it, even though his shirt was unbuttoned and flapped in the breeze. She was reminded of the first time she had seen him, watching the tide coming in on a beach thousands of miles away.

'So, he's the one. The Count you were telling me about.' There was no mistaking the bitterness in Alex's expression.

She nodded, biting her lip.

'He made you a vampire two hundred years ago and now he's here. Did you know he would be?'

'When we arrived, I . . . I sensed he might.'

Alex nodded. 'That's why you were so edgy about coming to Oakport.' She was shocked that he had noticed.

'I was scared about what would happen,' Ella said. She realized that she was scared now. Alex was slipping away from her and she was powerless to prevent it. She would only bring him pain. Maybe, if she left with Ethan, that would finally bring the Culler family a sense of peace.

'I'm leaving Oakport.'

Ella was stunned. She had been about to say the very same words.

'There's nothing for me here,' Alex continued. 'I'll leave in the morning. You can keep the car.'

For a second she considered suggesting that they left town immediately, together. But why was she kidding herself? It was over.

'I love you, Alex.'

He turned to look at her sadly and shrugged.

She could not blame him if he did not believe her. She could feel the tears pricking her eyes. Suddenly she couldn't bear to cry in front of him. She ran inside, into the bedroom and threw herself down on the bed. Why had she allowed this to happen? Why hadn't she just told Alex about Ethan as soon as she'd realized? In trying to protect him, she had only hurt him more.

She lay there in the darkness, wondering if Alex would come inside. If only he would give her a chance to explain. But what more could she say? Filled with despair, she submitted to sleep.

In the first moment of waking she felt refreshed and relaxed. She could feel the warmth of sunlight through the curtains. Opening her eyes, she turned to her side, just hoping. But Alex wasn't there.

An echo of the sadness she had felt the previous evening came to her. But it was displaced by another emotion. Sleep had brought her to a new decision. There was no more time to waste. She leapt out of bed.

The living room was empty. Maybe Alex had spent the whole night out on the deck. Ella approached the doors that led out to the lake. They were fastened. The deck was empty.

She looked into the bathroom. Empty. The kitchen. Nothing. Filled with panic, she pulled open the front door. The car was still there. Then she remembered him telling her that he'd leave her the car. Her heart was pounding as she shut the door again. It was then that she noticed the postcard on the table, weighted down by a ring of keys.

The card was picture side up. She picked it up. The picture of the small fishing port brought back a rush of memories of their travels. They'd eaten clam chowder that night, in an inn on the ocean-front. The memories flooded back. When she finally summoned the courage to turn over the card and read it, the sight of his spiky writing was too much to bear.

Be happy, love Alex.

Her tears spilled down on to the card, splattering the ink until the letters sprawled and twisted and were quite unreadable. Where had he gone? She had to find him. She had to tell him that it was him she loved, not Ethan. Even if he wouldn't take her back, she had to let him know.

She hammered on the door at Shadow Street for ages before anyone answered.

'I'm sorry, I was practising,' Charlie said. He was still holding his violin and bow.

'Is Alex here?'

Charlie shook his head.

'Was he here before?'

'Not this morning. Would you like to come inside? You look kind of upset.'

'Is Ethan here? Or Sarah?'

'Ethan's at his gallery and Sarah's gone into town.'

'I . . . have to find Alex . . .' Ella stammered.

'Sorry,' Charlie shrugged, 'I can't help you. Are you sure you don't want to come in?'

Standing there, wondering where to go next, Ella's eyes flashed over the photographs in the living room. There was one she hadn't noticed before. She darted inside. The scene the picture portrayed was familiar to her. It was the view from the living room of the boathouse. There was the deck, and beyond it the lake. There was the boat . . . the boat! It hadn't been there this morning. Alex must have taken it. Exhilarated by her discovery, she darted out of the house without offering Charlie any explanation. She had to get back to the boathouse. Nothing else mattered now.

When she arrived back at the boathouse, her exhilaration soon turned to frustration. The boat *had* gone but where had Alex taken it? She set off to search, on foot this time.

As she ran along the lakeside, her mind flooded with memories of Alex. The first time she had seen him, watching the waves. The first time they had kissed, alone on the beach. The terrible moment when his motorbike had veered off the cliff road and down . . . And then his smile as she had woken him from the sleep of death. She *had* to find him.

*

It was late afternoon when she finally returned to the boathouse after a long and futile search. She had not glimpsed the boat or Alex once. She felt bitterly disappointed.

There was so much she wanted to tell him. How it was always the same with Eduard. They'd come together for a while – he was exciting, there was no denying that. But to him, being a vampire was an excuse to take whatever he wanted – whoever he wanted – whatever the damage he wrought. And how he took life – or whatever this was – on the run.

Ella was tired of running. Eduard had told her that it was the only way. But she knew differently now. Since meeting Alex, a thousand new possibilities seemed to have opened up for her. With him, all the cynicism that had built up over 200 years had disappeared. She saw things freshly through his eyes. He might be a child compared to her and Ethan, but he had plenty to teach her just the same. She loved him – more than she would ever have thought possible. And now she missed him more than ever.

As she came to the door, she noticed a box propped to one side of the doorway. It hadn't been there that morning. She opened the door and carried it inside. Although large, it was quite light.

She carried it to the sofa and lifted the lid. There was a thick package wrapped in tissue paper. It rustled as she lifted it out from the box.

As the tissue fell away, she gasped. It was a green, silk dress – just like the one she had worn to that ball all those years before.

There was another package in the box. As if in a trance, she laid the dress carefully on the sofa and reached down into the box. A pair of emerald satin shoes tumbled out of their tissue wrapping. Spellbound, she dipped her feet into the slippers. They fitted perfectly.

At the very bottom of the box she found an envelope. As she lifted it closer, she saw that it was marked only 'E'. She took out the card inside and read the familiar writing: *What do you think? Not a bad likeness, is it? Wear it tonight and come to the gallery at eight.*

She set the card down and picked up the dress. Her thoughts were confused. She had to find Alex – had to focus on him not this dress, these slippers . . .

But suddenly, she found herself fastening the dress. She approached the mirror nervously, her eyes half-closed. The spell was complete.

She began pushing her hair into a different style. Now, when she examined the reflection, she no longer saw Ella Ryder. Princess Elisabeth had returned. All her thoughts turned to the ball that awaited her. She was impatient for the dance to begin. Impatient and nervous and excited.

CHAPTER XI

THE DOOR TO the gallery was open. She heard faint notes of music. As she stepped inside the music gained momentum.

She walked on through the hallway. Ahead of her, candles flickered. The light drew her on, until she was standing in the centre of the gallery. There were candlesticks and candelabra all around the edges of the room creating a moat of light.

The pictures she had viewed before had been removed from the walls. In their place were mirrors, of all shapes and sizes, reflecting the candles. As she struggled to distinguish the real candles from their reflections, she caught sight of him. He was dressed in a dark suit with tails. His face was covered by a mask.

'May I have this dance?' He held out his hand to her, but as she moved forward to take it, he appeared from another direction entirely. She realized that she had been watching him in the mirror. Now she trembled as he circled his arms around her.

She had not danced this way for a long time but her feet seemed to remember the steps. It was as if he had managed to turn time right back to the beginning.

As the music slowed she felt a sudden sense of sadness. He pulled her towards him and threw off the mask. His blond hair tumbled down around his neck.

She looked nervously into his eyes. He hesitated for a moment – his eyes taking in the way she looked in the dress, before returning to her face. His face came towards her then and she did not resist. His lips were upon hers and she reached out her hands to the back of his head and pulled him closer still.

They were still kissing as the waltz ended. As he drew away, he planted tiny kisses on her cheek and neck. She shivered, remembering what his kisses had brought her to before. But what more could he do to her now? Now they were equal. She smiled up at him as they began to dance again.

'What would you have done if I hadn't come?' she asked.

'I knew you would. You want this as much as I do.'

He was right. Everything else was only a distraction, an avoidance of the truth. The truth was simple. They should be together. Nothing else mattered.

She rested her head on his shoulder as they waltzed slowly around the room. But then, suddenly, she saw Charlie. At first she thought it was her imagination as he walked hesitantly towards her through the pool of light.

Ethan smiled. 'Charlie. We've been waiting for you.'

Ella was puzzled. What did he mean? Why had they been waiting for Charlie?

'Charlie's coming with us,' Ethan said, as if reading her mind.

'What? Why?' She was filled with confusion.

Ethan slipped his arm from her and moved towards Charlie. He stood behind him, resting his hands on the boy's shoulders.

'We're going to be a family.' He began stroking Charlie's hair. 'I have such plans for him.'

Ella suddenly felt cold. The spell was broken. She noticed with horror that Charlie's eyes were empty as glass.

'He'll make a better vampire than you or I,' Ethan said. 'He'll be a legend.'

Ella felt sick. This wasn't about love. It was about power. Nothing had changed. How could she have deceived herself? How could she have let him trick her once again?

'Ethan, I don't want Charlie to come with us. Let's just go together.'

He shook his head. 'Do you know how long I've been preparing this? I almost lost ... everything.'

'What do you mean?'

'When the boat went down,' he said, 'the water was pouring towards me. I only just made it to the dinghy in time. And then I had to rescue Charlie. I couldn't lose him then, after all those months of preparation.'

She held herself together, determined not to show her feelings. It was far from easy.

'You said it was an accident . . .'

'It *was* an accident,' Ethan said. 'But, of course, I saw the advantages. With no parents, no other family, there were no further obstacles. The plan could be accomplished.'

Ella glanced at Charlie. During all this, he remained quite impassive. Ethan had worked some kind of spell over him – just the way he had sent Alex to sleep that night at the boathouse. Just the way he had brought her here.

'So you left his parents to drown?' she said. 'And Alex.' She found it harder still to keep the emotion out of her voice.

He looked deep in thought, as if he had returned to that moment and was going through it all again.

'I thought about saving him. But it would only have complicated things. He would have stood in my way.'

'So you just left him there?'

'None of this matters now,' he said, pulling her towards him. 'I've made plans. We leave tonight . . .'

She drew back, slipping out of his arms. 'No,' she said, terrified but determined. 'I'm not coming.'

'Don't be foolish,' he said. 'You have no choice.'

She tensed her body, ready to run.

'Don't even think of it. This time, you won't get away from me.'

Perhaps he was right. Perhaps she should go with him, if only to protect Charlie. No. She would do everything in her power to stop him taking Charlie. She owed it to Alex. If only Alex were there now.

'Alex!' Charlie's voice called out.

Ella stared at Charlie, wondering how he had tuned into her thoughts. His eyes were fixed on the doors behind Ethan, the doors that gave out on to the dark waters of the lake.

She followed Charlie's gaze and saw Alex standing outside the window. Ethan saw him too. Suddenly Alex was in the room, standing before Ethan.

'Well, isn't this nice?' Ethan sneered. 'All vampires together!'

'All?' Alex faltered, staring at Charlie. 'What have you done?'

'We have to save Charlie!' Ella cried.

'You won't stop me! No one will stop me.' Ethan grabbed Charlie and held him in a vice-like grip.

Instinctively, Alex threw himself towards them. As he did so, he knocked one of the tall candlesticks. As it fell forward, the candles tumbled out and rolled across the floor towards the edges of the room. Ella watched them scatter in different directions. She ought to extinguish the flames but how could she reach them all in time?

Charlie was still caught in Ethan's grip. Alex struggled to free him but Ethan's hold only grew tighter. Ella saw the light glint on Ethan's teeth as his mouth lowered towards Charlie's neck.

'No!' she cried.

But her cries were drowned out by an explosion of noise and light. As the bright flash of the first fire gave way to thick black smoke, Ella could smell the stench of chemicals. The candles must have ignited some of Ethan's processing materials. She was submerged in a dark fog, broken only by flying glass as around her the mirrors caught fire and cracked.

She collapsed helplessly into a heap as the boathouse began to shake. She heard a terrible crash beside her. Looking up, she saw that the roof was starting to cave in. She had to get out to the lake. They all had to . . .

Her heart began to pound. She called out for Alex but had to close her mouth to stop the smoke from coming in. Petrified, she crawled across the floor, praying that she was moving in the right direction and not back into the heart of the fire.

As her hands reached the water, she felt a sudden rush of joy, but it soon died away, replaced by more practical concerns. She *had* to get inside the boat. She rolled inside, just as a new breath of fire lashed out at her. Quickly, she untied the boat from its mooring and took the oars in her hands. Her grip was poor but the current itself seemed to be carrying her away from the boathouse.

She looked up at the charred remains, searching frantically for the others. 'Alex!' she cried. The smoke had penetrated deep down into her throat and the cry sent a searing pain right through her. It didn't matter. The only thing that mattered was whether they were safe.

At last, two figures emerged from the smoke. She saw Charlie first. And behind him came Alex. Ella's heart lifted. It was a miracle. She steered the boat back towards the deck. Alex and Charlie staggered to the edge of the deck and jumped down beside her.

The building was utterly consumed by fire. Where was Ethan? Ella's blood ran cold. After everything he had done to her – to them all – she still felt a wrench of pain as she saw the billowing smoke.

Suddenly, he appeared. He looked weak and fearful. She had never seen him this way.

'Come on!' she cried instinctively. 'Get into the boat!'

He looked at her strangely. It was as if he did not know her. He seemed unable to move, rooted to the spot. Ella had to turn her eyes as the last remains of the ceiling caved in and he was crushed under a blanket of fire.

She screamed. Alex grabbed the oars and began rowing them away from shore. Once they had gone a safe distance, he let the oars drop and took Ella in his arms. Tears were streaming down her face and she was shaking.

'It's OK,' Alex whispered. 'Everything's going to be OK.'

Ella pulled Alex's face towards her and kissed him. It had taken this to bring them back together. Now, she never wanted them to be apart again. She tried to tell him but he hushed her. Well, there would be time enough to tell him how she felt.

They moored the boat further up the lake. She could hear the sirens as fire trucks made their way through the night. It was too late, she thought ruefully. Too late for Ethan Sawyer.

Even as she saw the flames take their final hold on the deck, Ella found it hard to believe that he was gone. And that he was never coming back. She felt a surge of regret. She had loved him. She could no longer deny it.

And yet, he had been a savage man. Evil. His final actions on earth had shown that. She turned to Charlie. His neck was still red where Ethan had held him in his deathly grip. Charlie smiled up at her. He looked different somehow, as if the shock and terror had broken Ethan's spell.

'Thank you,' he said. 'You saved us.'

Ella felt Alex's arms circling her waist. Felt his lips brush against her neck. She leaned back against him, her eyes lifting towards the dark sky. Though she was still shaking and full of fear, she knew that there was one thing she could be sure of – Alex loved her. And she loved him. And, whatever other dragons lay in wait for them, they would face them and fight them. Together.

Also in the DARK ENCHANTMENT series

Firespell
by LOUISE COOPER

CHAPTER I

PRIDDY CAME INTO the turret room that Lianne shared with her sister, Gretala, and her voice was very quiet as she said, 'Your grandmother wants to see you.'

Lianne and Gretala exchanged an uneasy look. Grandmother had been ill for some time, and lately the servants had begun to whisper that her sickness was growing worse. The apothecary called every day, and there was a sinister hush in the west wing where Grandmother's room was. Now, seeing their old nurse's serious face, the girls knew the truth.

'Yes,' Priddy nodded sombrely. 'Your grandmother is dying. The apothecary says she will make the great journey before nightfall, so you must go to her and say your goodbyes.' She beckoned them towards the door. 'Come along, now.'

Lianne's face grew stricken. 'To the west wing . . .?' she whispered.

'Yes.' Then Priddy's expression softened. 'There's nothing to fear there. Only shadows, and they can't hurt anyone. Come, now. No dawdling.'

Lianne tried very hard not to think about shadows as she and Gretala followed Priddy's bobbing candle to the west wing. The corridors were chill and gloomy, and outside the wind was rising. It moaned eerily, and all the windows had started to rattle, as if a hundred ghouls were trying to prise them open and get into the house. On the walls, portraits of the Cerne family ancestors watched the girls hurry by. Lianne didn't dare look at the faces in the pictures. They were all grim in the brightest daylight; on this hideous autumn evening they would be nightmarish.

Lord and Lady Cerne were waiting outside Grandmother's door. Lady Cerne looked as if she had been crying, and Lord Cerne didn't greet his daughters but only said, 'Your grandmother is waiting for you. She wants to see you one at a time. Lianne, you are to go first.'

Lianne's heart missed a beat. She didn't want

to be first, and she looked at Gretala in appeal. But Lord Cerne frowned and said sternly, 'Lianne, did you hear me?'

She swallowed and dropped an obedient curtsy. 'Yes, Father.' And, taking a deep breath, she reached out for the door handle.

'Lianne . . . is that Lianne?'

The voice sounded like the rustling of dead leaves, so feeble and thin that Lianne could barely hear it. 'Yes, Grandmother,' she whispered back.

'Ah, I can see your hair now. Your handsome auburn hair . . . Come closer, child. Stand in the light, where I can also see your face.'

Lianne tiptoed towards the huge, curtained bed. Six candles burned in a branched sconce on a table, but the light they gave was weak and pale. An elderly maid sat in a chair by the empty fireplace, apparently asleep. The room was very cold. And the wind outside was howling now, like a damned soul.

Grandmother lay propped up by pillows, looking tiny and lost among all the whiteness. Lianne dropped a deeper curtsy. She felt she should say something but couldn't find any words. Besides, she had always been terrified of Grandmother, with her sharp tongue, cold grey eyes and harsh face. Everyone was terrified of Grandmother, and always had been.

But soon, she thought, there would be nothing left to fear. For Grandmother would be just another shadow . . .

An old, withered hand, like a bird's claw, moved across the counterpane, and Grandmother's fingers curled round a black wood box that lay just within reach. 'I have something for you, Lianne,' she said. 'A gift. I want you to keep it always, so whenever you look at it or wear it, you will remember me and say a prayer for my soul.'

Her words sent a cold shiver through Lianne but she tried not to show it. 'Yes Grandmother,' she said again. 'I will.'

'Good. Good.' The lid of the box opened with an unpleasant creaking sound. Grandmother fumbled inside, then drew something out. 'Here, child.'

It was a bracelet. Lianne had seen it before, for it was one of Grandmother's favourites and she always wore it on special occasions. The last such occasion, Lianne remembered, had been the Midsummer banquet in the great hall downstairs. Each year the wealthy families of the district took turns to host the Midsummer feast; this year it had been their turn and there had been rare merriment in Cerne House. Sir Han Carler's son had been very attentive to Gretala that night. Grandmother had disapproved, and the girls had laughed about it afterwards –

The old woman's voice cut across her thoughts. 'Next year, you shall be the one to wear the bracelet. And you will do so in memory of me.'

Startled, Lianne blinked as she realized that Grandmother had read her thoughts. She had always had that uncanny ability. It was frightening . . .

Slowly, she took the bracelet. It was silver, and studded with sapphires. They were cold gems, Lianne thought, as cold as Grandmother, and the idea of wearing them made her shudder inwardly. But she was careful not to let her feelings show as she said, 'Thank you, Grandmother. You are very . . . kind.'

Grandmother had never been kind in her life, but her sunken mouth moved in a sour little smile. 'Go now,' she said. 'And send your sister to me.' She paused. 'You will not see me again, Lianne.'

Lianne was seized with a fear that she would have to kiss Grandmother's wizened cheek, but to her relief the old woman didn't seem to expect it. Nor did Grandmother say goodbye, or give her a blessing; in fact she said nothing more at all, only waved that claw-like hand, dismissing Lianne from the room.

They were all waiting outside: Lord and Lady Cerne, Gretala and Priddy. Gretala went nervously into the bedroom, and though Lianne tried to hear what Grandmother might be saying to her, the only sound that came was the moaning of the wind. Priddy clucked over the sapphire bracelet, but Lord and Lady Cerne showed no interest. They seemed uneasy, as though they were waiting for something unpleasant to happen. And then Gretala emerged.

She was carrying a small, velvet-covered box, and there was a frown on her pretty face. Lady Cerne tensed instantly and would have spoken, but her husband touched her arm.

'No, wife. Not here.' He turned suddenly to the nurse. 'Priddy, take Miss Lianne back to her room.' And, seeing that Lianne was about to object, he added ferociously, '*Now*, woman! Do you hear me?'

Priddy bridled but didn't dare argue. She caught hold of Lianne's arm so hard that her fingers pinched, and replied a little huffily, 'Of course, My Lord. If you say so.'

'But Father —' Lianne began. Priddy shook her and, knowing it was a warning, she fell silent. But she looked back over her shoulder as the nurse hurried her away. Her parents were talking to Gretala, urgently, or so it seemed. Lianne couldn't tell what the conversation was about, but as the wind lulled momentarily one snatch did reach her ears. Her father's voice. And what he said made Lianne's skin crawl.

'Oh, yes. Oh, yes. This is what I had feared . . .'

'Now, however should I know what His Lordship wanted to say to your sister?' Priddy closed the shutters of the turret bedroom, then moved to the fire and began to rake the logs with unnecessary vigour. She had her self-righteous look on, and Lianne knew she was still bristling over Lord Cerne's curt dismissal. 'It's not my place to ask.' She looked up. 'And neither is it yours.'

Lianne pouted. 'I only wanted to know what gift Grandmother gave to Gretala. There was no need for Father to speak so harshly.' She sighed, and sat down on her bed. 'But then he always is harsh. He always has been.'

Priddy's face softened a little, for she had been with the family for nearly fifty years and had been nurse to Lord Cerne himself when he was small. 'Not always, Lianne,' she said gently. 'He was different once. A long time ago. But time changes people. And this has never been a happy house.'

As if echoing those last words, the voice of the wind rose suddenly to a doleful wail. The shutters rattled violently and Lianne shivered and hugged herself.

'I wish I could leave, Priddy. I wish I could marry and go away from this house for ever.'

'Now, now,' Priddy chided. 'You're only fifteen; that's too young to think about such things.'

'It isn't too young. Gretala's only two years older, and Mother says she'll probably be betrothed soon.'

'Betrothed's one thing, married's another,' Priddy said, then relented a little. 'Don't fret. Plenty of time for you to find a handsome young man.'

Lianne gave her an odd look. 'Before Cerne House works its dark magic on me, too?'

'Now, I didn't say that.'

'But it's true, isn't it?' Lianne persisted. 'Tezer says there's a curse on this house and everyone in it.'

'Tezer's a fool who should know better than to go spreading rumours,' Priddy retorted. 'And *you*, Miss, shouldn't spend your time in the company of the stable servants! What would your father say if he knew?'

Lianne shrugged. 'He doesn't know. And he won't find out unless you tell him.' She paused. 'But *is* it true, Priddy? About a curse?'

'I'm sure I've no idea.' Priddy's mouth snapped shut so fast and firmly that Lianne knew she was lying. But before Lianne could persevere, the nurse came bustling back to the bed. 'Up from there, now. Your sister will be back at any moment, and then you must both spend an hour at your history.'

'Oh, *Priddy* –'

'A proper lady must be knowledgeable as well as decorative,' said Priddy. 'How can you hope to snare that handsome husband you long for, if you have no learning?'

It was impossible to argue with Priddy's logic when she was in this mood, and Lianne gave in. 'Very well, if I *must*.'

'And put that bracelet away.' Lianne had dropped Grandmother's gift on the bed beside her. 'It isn't respectful just to leave it lying there as it is.'

Lianne frowned. 'I don't like it. I wish Grandmother had chosen to give me something else.'

'Doubtless she had her own good reasons, and it isn't for us to question them. Though I must say that warmer stones would have suited you better. Rubies, maybe. Sapphires are much more your sister's colour, for they match her eyes and set off all that handsome black hair. Now,' Priddy brushed her hands together, making it clear that she was determined to change the subject, 'fetch your books and get ready for your studies. When your sister –'

She stopped, as suddenly a new sound mingled with the wind's wail. The shutters and the turret's thick stone walls muffled it, but they both recognized it instantly. Slowly, mournfully, the great bell that hung in the central tower of Cerne House had begun to toll.

Lianne started to her feet and whispered, '*Grandmother . . .*'

Priddy was listening to the bell and her face had taken on a strange look. At last she spoke. 'Your grandmother is dead.' She shut her eyes. 'Rest her soul.'

And in her voice, Lianne thought, was relief . . . and fear.

Blood Dance

by LOUISE COOPER

Garland expects her betrothal to the man she loves to bring her happiness. But her new life is threatened by a dark, supernatural power from which there seems to be no escape – unless she can find the answer to a long-lost secret.

Also in **DARK ENCHANTMENT**

Firespell

by LOUISE COOPER

When Lianne looks into the heart of
the topaz, she discovers the man she is
to fall in love with – and at the same
time reawakens an old family curse. But
is the handsome face that beckons her
from within the jewel one of good or
evil? Is he from this world or the next?
And can Lianne's love ever win?

Also in **DARK ENCHANTMENT**

The Hounds of Winter

by LOUISE COOPER

Tavia's marriage to a handsome but mysterious aristocrat kindles her sister Jansie's jealousy – but it also awakens a sinister force. For, as the first snow falls, the hounds of winter are unleashed and danger closes in. Can Jansie save her sister and herself?

Also in DARK ENCHANTMENT

House of Thorns

by JUDY DELAGHTY

When Elaine and Gwen seek their
fortunes in the gypsy camp, Elaine's
destiny is woven into a dark mystery.
Will she be forced to marry Peter,
Heir of Thorncliffe, or can she find
a magical way to escape?

Also in DARK ENCHANTMENT

Kiss of the Vampire

by J. B. CALCHMAN

The ancient town of St Doves rarely welcomes strangers and the arrival of Alex Culler, tall, dark, mysterious and ageless, reawakens superstitions that should have been dead and buried. Why is it, when she could have anyone, Ella wants Alex? And why is it he seems to find her just as irresistible?

Also in DARK ENCHANTMENT

The Lost Brides

by THERESA RADCLIFFE

When the beautiful orphan Catherine returns to the old forgotten family seat of Helmsby Abbey, strange secrets from the past lie in wait amongst the ruins – as well as unexpected romance. Helmsby Abbey is a place where love has always ended in tragedy, but can Catherine be the first to escape?

Also in DARK ENCHANTMENT

The Shrouded Mirror

by LOUISE COOPER

Aline's arrival at the home of the wealthy Orielle and her brother Orlando promises to bring her friendship and love. So why does Aline begin to suffer terrible nightmares and who is it that torments her at night with whispered taunts? How can she fight back when the nightmare reaches from another world to snatch her happiness away?

Also in DARK ENCHANTMENT

Valley of Wolves

by THERESA RADCLIFFE

Every winter the wolves come down
from the mountains in search of food.
Every winter Marie remembers how she
lost her father and Jean-Pierre, the boy
she loved. But now she has been told
Jean-Pierre has returned from the dead.
And now the howling of wolves comes
from inside the château.

READ MORE IN PUFFIN

For children of all ages, Puffin represents quality and variety – the very best in publishing today around the world.

For complete information about books available from Puffin – and Penguin – and how to order them, contact us at the appropriate address below. Please note that for copyright reasons the selection of books varies from country to country.

On the world wide web: www.penguin.co.uk

In the United Kingdom: Please write to *Dept. EP, Penguin Books Ltd, Bath Road, Harmondsworth, West Drayton, Middlesex UB7 0DA*

In the United States: Please write to *Consumer Sales, Penguin USA, P.O. Box 999, Dept. 17109, Bergenfield, New Jersey 07621-0120.* VISA and MasterCard holders call 1-800-253-6476 to order Penguin titles

In Canada: Please write to *Penguin Books Canada Ltd, 10 Alcorn Avenue, Suite 300, Toronto, Ontario M4V 3B2*

In Australia: Please write to *Penguin Books Australia Ltd, P.O. Box 257, Ringwood, Victoria 3134*

In New Zealand: Please write to *Penguin Books (NZ) Ltd, Private Bag 102902, North Shore Mail Centre, Auckland 10*

In India: Please write to *Penguin Books India Pvt Ltd, 706 Eros Apartments, 56 Nehru Place, New Delhi 110 019*

In the Netherlands: Please write to *Penguin Books Netherlands bv, Postbus 3507, NL-1001 AH Amsterdam*

In Germany: Please write to *Penguin Books Deutschland GmbH, Metzlerstrasse 26, 60594 Frankfurt am Main*

In Spain: Please write to *Penguin Books S. A., Bravo Murillo 19, 1° B, 28015 Madrid*

In Italy: Please write to *Penguin Italia s.r.l., Via Felice Casati 20, I–20124 Milano*

In France: Please write to *Penguin France S. A., 17 rue Lejeune, F–31000 Toulouse*

In Japan: Please write to *Penguin Books Japan, Ishikiribashi Building, 2–5–4, Suido, Bunkyo-ku, Tokyo 112*

In South Africa: Please write to *Longman Penguin Southern Africa (Pty) Ltd, Private Bag X08, Bertsham 2013*